Rouse
The Crowd

How to interact with audiences for gigs they can't forget

Written by Gareth Bird

http://www.gig-getter.com

GBA Publishing
GBA Publishing, 52 Walton Road, Stockton Heath, Cheshire, WA4 6NL

ISBN: 978-0-9562554-1-9

Printed in the United Kingdom

CONTENTS

PART 2: **When you're on stage – Crowd Rousing**

Introduction

You've won the gig, but what about the crowd?

If you're gigging regularly you should give yourself a pat on the back. Seriously. There are hundreds of thousands of bands, millions of musicians who will never know that level of success. Many who try to start bands will have little or no success with gigs. Plenty who do play live will eventually give up through audience indifference.

Overcoming this audience indifference or lack of interest is what *Rouse the Crowd* is all about.

Maybe you're one of the millions who's learnt your instrument to some degree but never go out of the house with it. Perhaps you're fearful of playing in front of other people. If that's you, then *Rouse the Crowd* will show you how you can join the ranks of successful musical performers.

Whatever your gigging situation at the moment, you'll discover how to turn your every live performance in a bar, club or at a private party from another instantly forgettable couple of hours into something special that fixes itself in people's minds for a long time after. How to help you get the people who see you live to work on your behalf, talking about your gigs for days after to anyone who will listen.

You're going to discover hundreds of ideas which will help you to improve the gigs you play by getting your crowds going. Whipping them up, getting them excited and involved with you. There are ideas for what you can say and do on stage over and above your music, to make a real connection with every audience you play to. A connection which will turn your gigs into rare and unforgettable events. The result will be more and better repeat bookings, more private parties, a larger fan base and a great night every time for your audience and for you.

Some of these techniques come from my own personal experience playing places like the *Hard Rock Café*. I've been a regular performer there since 2004. I've played hundreds of gigs in bars, clubs and private functions. I've also written about gigging for Future Publishing's *Total Guitar Magazine, Bass Guitar Magazine* and numerous online publications.

Other ideas you'll learn come from the most effective and successful performers and crowd rousers on the semi-pro music scene. Many of these are readers of my first manual about gigging, *Gig-Getter: How to get more gigs than you can play.* Gig-Getter (www.gig-getter.com) has so far been used by musicians in more than 15 countries around the world and has been a top-selling guide to getting gigs on Amazon in the UK since it first appeared there in 2009.

You'll also find inspiration from hundreds of hours spent researching entertainers and performers outside the world of music. Their ideas have been adapted and tested for success for bands and solo artists like you and I.

Rouse the Crowd is something of a missing link. It's something I started exploring in 2007 when my band lost its wild extrovert front man. His antics and natural ability to get crowds involved during our gigs were a large part of our success, what made us stand out and for us being one of only a handful of bands on the regular roster at places like the *Hard Rock*.

The best replacement we could find in time for our relentless gig schedule was perfect in terms of musical and vocal ability. However, he was a quiet introvert and it quickly became apparent how much we'd relied on our ex front man for audience interaction. We desperately needed an injection of "personality" to get some excitement back into gig nights and get crowds responding to us again or there would be trouble ahead...

By putting together a plan from all the acts I studied, we were able to turn our performances around quite spectacularly and the band went from strength to strength. Since then this system you're about to learn has been tested with repeated success for semi-pro bands and solo artists around the world. This means you can be confident this system can work for you too, even if you've never gigged before.

A word of warning: There are musicians who will tell you to forget any form of communication with your audience other than your music. Remember, no gig is ever *only* about the music. However, it is fair to say that no amount of know-how about what to say to a crowd or what moves to pull will save you if you can't play, if you're not rehearsed, if your material choice is lousy or if your gear doesn't work properly. So, we'll assume these basics are pretty much covered though you will find some further ideas about rehearsing and material inside this manual.

The information in *Rouse the Crowd* is arranged into two key parts. Firstly comes the preparation needed before you get up on stage to successfully interact with an audience. This includes *analysing your current performances* (if you're already gigging) and deciding exactly *what sort of show you want to put on.* Most importantly, this first part of the manual includes *developing the confidence* you'll need to get a crowd going.

The second part of the manual covers the specific techniques you can use on stage. It includes *how to recognise the most receptive audience members* at any gig – to get the whole crowd going. You'll understand the most effective ways for each type of musician or singer to move on stage. *How and when to talk to an audience* and to engage them in ways guaranteed to help you go down great whenever you play. All of this is designed to help you to get asked back by the venue time after time.

Finally, I should say that I'm well aware that many musicians are introverted and not natural "performers" - I'm one of them. So, I've also included plenty of tips and exercises to help greatly with your self-confidence on stage. Ideas to free you up from worrying about playing or other technical considerations so you can concentrate, when needed, on the audience interaction aspects of your gigs.

So, let's get started.

PART 1: **Before you get on stage - Preparation**

1. Your fast first step - Take a look at your act now

2. Just how roused do you want your crowds?

3. How to create confidence to *"Get in their faces"*

4. Your crowd-rousing plan – Start with your set list

Step 1: **Your fast first step - Take a look at your act now**

1.1 Start recording your act

First we need to take stock of your current position and consider that versus what it takes to get audiences involved and excited. You need to understand if and how you're engaging your crowds before you can look at trying to improve this.

Assuming you're already gigging and happy with the musical side of things, start by videoing your next couple of performances. Ideally you'll have someone filming who can move around and film all band members from the perspective of the audience. If not, just put the camera down on a table (somewhere you can keep your eye on it) in a fixed position where it can see the whole of the band. A camera tripod would be ideal if you have one.

If you're not gigging yet, record a rehearsal as if it's a gig. Push through feeling self-conscious or foolish and play your sets while pretending the camera is a crowd.

The main thing is to do what most bands don't do when they watch themselves back. You're not focusing on the quality of your music with this exercise. You're looking at the appearance, movement and interaction, especially talking, with your audience. Ask yourself whether you would hold your own attention if you were in the audience. We did this when we first began playing without our original extrovert front man and were getting indifferent crowd reactions. The

11

recordings were painful to watch. There was little, if any, movement on stage and a lot of staring at fret boards.

So, study each band member and their contribution to both the visual and interaction side of things.

Is the way they look saying the kind of things you want it to about the band? Who's moving around? How? Note down anything that strikes you at this time. Take a note of any on mic talking, the exact words and phrases and where they're said during the gig. Are there any dead spaces or embarrassing silences in between songs? All of this will come in useful later on.

If you really don't think you have access to a video recorder - are you sure? At least some of a performance could be recorded even if only filmed with a phone? But if you draw a blank you can record the sound only. Concentrate on the talking and gaps between songs as mentioned above. What particular phrases or moments, if any, seemed to get a positive crowd reaction from what you could hear?

As you'll see in Step 5, a great deal of the image and communication you can achieve is a result of the way you look. So without studying your current visual impact you'll be selling yourself short.

There is a way around this though.

1.2 **It's all done with mirrors**

Just like when you were a kid in your bedroom dreaming of playing on stage, mirrors can form a useful part of your analysis – whether you have a video to start with or not.

When researching stage presence and audience interaction I actually found a number of performers recommending rehearsing in front of a large mirror. To get any real benefit from this though, you've got to move around at rehearsal as you would do on stage. In an ideal world the whole band would do this together with a mirror or mirrors that are big enough.

In reality, this is difficult to achieve unless you know someone who works in a mirror factory. So, the likelihood is, you'll need to practise on your own at home, in the mirror.

In the group rehearsal scenario, you could still all move about as you would on stage and everyone critiques each other. Remember at this point, all you're looking for is how you're doing at the moment; you're not yet trying to put that right.

The key here is that you **have** to understand how you look, move and sound before you can improve it and you're going to need to see yourself the way other people do before this can happen. More about this later.

If you're gigging frequently, record a few gigs to give yourself a better picture of your current performance.

In the next step, having looked at your current behaviour when playing, we need to think about what impact you want to have on your crowds. What sort of audience interaction you're aiming for...

Step 2:   Just how roused do you want your crowds?

By now you should have some idea of how you currently come across to crowds. Next, you need to decide *how* you want this to improve.

2.1   What sort of image and interaction do you want?

You won't create the sort of rapport you want with audiences until you decide precisely on what it is you want to achieve. How exactly do you want to come across? Making sure the people watching you have an enjoyable and entertaining time is a good place to start. It might sound obvious, but thinking about what the audience wants is different from being focused solely on playing your parts well. Even if all you want to do is to aim to give them something more to watch than four figures staring at their kit or fret boards.

It may be that you don't feel you need radical changes. Perhaps you just want to be able to comfortably chat to the crowd a little in between songs so that there's some sort of response or acknowledgement from them. Or maybe you want to take it to the other extreme, getting them up on stage or joining in with the band. Keep in mind that it's likely what you want to achieve with your crowd interaction may differ from time to time with the types of gigs you play; bars, clubs, private functions etc.

Either way, think about how you want your gigs to be

different from what you saw of yourselves on video.

Whatever you want to achieve, try where you can to involve all band members in this discussion. Sometimes other members may be reluctant to do this, especially if they have the "*It's all about the music*" mentality.

If this is the case, and you're determined to stick with this band and these band mates, fear not. One person alone making changes can still make a big difference – even if it's not the one at the front of the stage.

2.2   If it's good enough for "Battle of the Bands..."

Competitions known as "Battle of the Bands" first became a pop culture favourite in the 1960s and I'm sure you're familiar with the idea of them.

To help you persuade reluctant band members, or just to help focus your own thinking, look here at the "*Interface with audience*" section from the criteria for a typical Battle of the Bands competition like you may have come across yourself:

Interface with audience

- *Verbal Interaction:*
  Did the band introduce themselves at all? Did the band talk to or with the audience?

- *Physical Interaction:*
  Did the band physically participate with the audience e.g. Eye contact, head nod, gesturing,

acknowledgements, waving, dancing with the audience or giving hand signals?

- *Confidence*:
  Was the band confident in their interaction with the audience?

- *Appearance*:
  Did the band show personality on stage? Did the band appear to enjoy what they were doing?

- *Entertainment factor/Showmanship*:
  Did the band entertain? Did one or the entire band display showmanship towards the crowd?

This is useful food for thought even if you've never had any intention of competing in anything like this. You can see what factors professional judges consider important for a band. These are the aspects you should keep in mind as you look at establishing your own on stage identity and presence.

2.3   **What's everyone else doing?**

You can add to your thinking here on the road to defining your own goals by studying some of your favourite bands and performers on sites like youtube. You don't need to slavishly copy them. Just get some ideas and adapt what you see and hear for your own act. Keep in mind that most of these acts will be playing to audiences who are already devoted followers. This is probably not the case with you – yet.

Also, you should go and watch other local acts, those you may be competing with for venues. Watch exactly what they do in terms of audience interaction and how it compares with you. This is very different from checking out whether their guitarist is faster around the fret board than you are. All this will go to help with your thinking and the development of your own audience interaction.

As you realise now, knowing the state of the crowd responses you usually get and what you want that to change to is a crucial part of the planning process. But this knowledge alone won't make you great with your audience. What if the thought of trying to engage the crowd scares you senseless? A lot of musicians are not natural extroverts. This doesn't matter. What does matter is that it can be overcome. In the next step you'll see plenty of ideas for how.

Step 3: How to create confidence to "*Get in their faces*"

3.1 Break free from the music

If you're scared at the thought of looking up and out towards your crowds, no matter how small a number may be watching, you're not alone. But this can be overcome.

The first essential point is to make sure you're on top of the music. This is the physical or technical side of self-confidence. Like the footballer who needs to make sure he's match fit and knows who to mark and where to aim his free kicks in any particular game.

Playing live, you can't really spend any time focusing on what to say to the crowd, or how you move, if you're worried about the words in the next line of the lyrics or whether you can actually play that solo which is approaching.

So, boring as it may sound, you have to practise, practise and practise so you can play almost without thinking. Here are some ideas to accelerate this and to make you better than you'll probably actually need to be on stage.

- *Practise as if playing live*
To really get comfortable with your material and, over time, reduce how much you need to think about what you're doing, rehearse *as if* you were gigging. This means sticking to the set list in terms of which songs and the order you rehearse them. You can work out song starts (who does what), where there are potential problem areas (down-

19

tunings, guitar switches etc).

More on this in Step 4.

You might also find yourself coming up with ideas for things to say or do while playing in a more relaxed frame of mind at rehearsal. Don't let these inspired moments escape. Make a note of any thoughts. As time goes on and you build up a few ideas of things you could say to the crowd in certain places in the set or maybe some moves you could make, (see Step 10 for more info) you can even slip them into your rehearsal routine.

Playing the set list when you're practising is the same as a "dress rehearsal" and will itself help ease any stress on gig-night. You'll have been through the same songs in the same order countless times before. This will increase your confidence and technical mastery just like playing gig after gig.

- *Phrase Trainers*
It's all very well rehearsing as a band, but what if these sessions aren't as regular or as long as you'd like or feel you need?

If you've read Gig-getter you'll know I'm a big fan of Phrase Trainers. No bigger than an iPod, these great little tools let you rehearse alone without waiting for the next band get-together. You can get them for guitarists, bassists and even vocalists. (Drummers and keyboard players please write stiff letters to the companies mentioned on the next page.)

Basically, you can take a recording of your band playing their sets (or use MP3s of the originals if you're a cover act), mute your part on the recording and jam along – as if rehearsing with the band concerned. The newer models even have a recording feature to enable you to listen to how much better all this additional private rehearsal is making you. You can even record any ideas you might have for audience banter as they occur to you.

Here are links to two of the most popular models on the market:

My personal preference is the *Tascam* brand:
www.tascam.com/products/gt-r1.html
This particular model is for guitarists and bassists but you'll find other units for vocalists on the same site.

Boss also has a great reputation though:
www.rolandus.com/products/productdetails.aspx?ObjectId=818

You will find others if you check Google.

Playing along with your band or better still your heroes while you sit on the sofa sipping a beer? Monday nights don't get much better than that, do they?

The money you spend on one of these trainers can be the greatest musical investment you'll ever make to improve your playing and free you up to focus on the crowd while on stage.

- *Handicap yourself: practise in the dark*
You can do this in a full band situation if you don't feel too daft about it and you think there's no danger of falling over each other. Probably, it's best to keep this option to when you're running through the songs alone at home. You can do this literally or a less radical method, would be to simply

not look at what your arms or fingers are playing (or studying the lyric sheets) while you rehearse.

Either way, as you push yourself to spend more and more time playing without watching what you're doing, you can be looking up and outward at the crowd instead when on stage.

How else could you handicap yourself?

- *Weigh yourself down: resistance training*
This technique works in a similar way to the darkness idea, in that you make your playing harder for yourself in rehearsal. Like someone in the armed forces or a serious runner may burden themselves with weights in their backpack or on their ankles when they run or train, you weigh down your wrists.

Some guitarists do this as a matter of course wearing a heavy watch and / or wristbands on their fretting hand when they rehearse. The wrist is left bare and so lighter whenever they play live.

A final thought on making life tougher for yourself in rehearsal comes from a bassist in one punk band I know. He complained that he always had to stay stone cold sober or he couldn't be sure he wouldn't make mistakes with his playing (not very "punky" when you think about it). Anyhow, his lead guitarist (an accomplished drinker) took issue with this, insisting that the bassist should practise at home when extremely drunk and record the performance.

Only when he had mastered rehearsing while drunk could he be confident enough to do it for real. Well, that's one way of handicapping yourself I suppose - but not one I particularly recommend.

The idea with any of these more sensible techniques is to make playing feel so much easier on gig night and so increase your confidence. Ultimately leaving you free to focus more on interacting with the audience.

3.2   Developing *inner* performance confidence

There are a couple of fundamental keys to developing the right attitude before and when you go on stage:

- *Keep your focus on **them** not you*
Remember that every performance should be about *"giving"* a good time to the crowd rather than *"taking"* their approval, applause or admiration. This may seem a strange thing to say, but it's actually very important. Keeping it in mind will influence your behaviour and feelings on stage and so help you with your ability to "rouse the crowd".

- *Some people (audience members) may need help and encouragement to really enjoy themselves*
Not everyone can automatically let go and have a great time when they go out. Helping them do so is where you need to come in.

Carl, a young singer songwriter who's trying to make a name for himself as a solo artist, described the fear that descended over him when he first started playing in public as being like: *"Time standing still"*. He said he felt that every move of each part of his body, his facial expressions and every note he played were being examined by the whole room.

I smiled when I read this as I can remember feeling exactly the same myself in the early days of playing live.

If that sounds familiar to you and you suffer from any form of performance anxiety here are some tools that will help you.

Even if you're gigging reasonably comfortably, simply implementing any of these techniques which might appeal to you can boost your confidence, make you come out of your shell more and so help you put on a greater show for the people who are watching.

- *Instant relaxation*
I've studied and trained in relaxation for over twenty years and know that tension can be useful at certain times. On stage though, you'll generally perform and relate to your audiences better if you're feeling relaxed. Two simple techniques you can use are:

- *Breathe deeply and slowly*
Just become aware of your breathing pattern, as this is a key to your feelings of either tension or relaxation. Once you're aware of it, just deepen it and slow it down. The beauty of this is that it will naturally dissolve feelings of tension and replace them with calmness. You will have to keep on top of it as you're learning, repeat it over and over. But it will eventually become natural and work for you.

- *Loosen your muscles*
As well as your breathing, tension is transmitted in particular to your muscles. They'll become tight and this will amplify your feelings of stress. Tension in the shoulders can be a particular issue for a musician, interfering with smooth and unrestricted playing.

Try to stay aware of when your muscles are tightening up and loosen them. Slacken them on purpose. You don't need to stand there and try to turn yourself into a jellyfish. When you concentrate on areas like your *shoulders,* for example, be aware that they can tend to rise up towards your head and stiffen when you're anxious – so be on guard for this happening.

Lower your shoulders and move them around a little to loosen them. You can do this discreetly; it doesn't have to be done in a big theatrical way - although perhaps it's the missing stage move you've been searching for! However, you might want to stop the technique if you're getting some funny looks because of it.

Other key areas in most people are the *jaws,* the *teeth* and the *tongue,* all of which have a tendency to clamp together when you're tense. Not great if you're a singer as you can imagine. Any time a voice has sounded unusually thin and reedy is generally a result of this kind of tension.

If this is a problem you have, to deal with this just be conscious of your mouth and make sure your top and bottom teeth are separated a little (as opposed to grinding together). Check your tongue isn't pressed up into the roof of your mouth; let it sit limply in the bottom of your mouth.

Many musicians, when they study early videos of themselves at gigs, realise tension is transmitted in the face. This results in an almost permanent frown. Not a great look or one likely to generate any feelings of warmth in those standing opposite the stage looking at you. Once you're aware of the issue you'll be able to "police" yourself and keep the frown from your face.

3.3 **Fake it 'til you make it**

A musician from London tells the story about a course he did in music business promotion a few years ago at college. One of his lecturers was a guy from the North of the UK who'd been a pro musician in the 60's and 70's. The lecturer told his students about once watching a singer backstage in the early 1960's when they were gigging in London. This singer was standing in front of a full-length mirror, pulling poses and prancing around telling himself out loud:

"You are the f****** man, you own the stage!"

and such like. The lecturer said that he and the rest of his band were laughing at this *"little poser"* and thought he was a bit of a clown.

However, the "little poser" then went out on stage and blew the place away. He performed all the movements and gestures on stage that he'd been practising in front of that mirror minutes before and the crowd had gone wild. It looked completely natural and off the cuff on stage – but of course it wasn't. And that was the point.

The lecturer went on to mention that the "little poser" is still performing today as front man / senior citizen in one of the biggest rock bands of all time....

There's actually scientific research that backs up why this kind of preparation for going on stage worked for that singer in the mirror I just described.

You may have come across something called **NLP** or *Neuro Linguistic Programming*. It's basically a system of changing the way you feel and behave which started out originally as a study of psychotherapists in California in the 1970's. It's gone on to achieve worldwide acclaim as a system, and has helped people transform the way they think, behave and communicate. It's used in the work of people like Tony Robbins in the States and Paul McKenna in the UK.

There's one particular NLP technique which musicians can use that will quickly transform the way you feel about any performance. It can help you to think and behave the way you'd like to on stage.

NLP practitioners believe that every feeling or emotion (like happiness, sadness, confidence or anxiety for example) which we feel has, over time, developed a set of physical positions or movements which are always associated with it. So, for example, when you're sad or depressed you'll tend to adopt the same certain physical mannerisms each time. Commonly feeling depressed or unhappy will result in a head being bowed to some extent, looking downward and not smiling, for instance.

Think about it yourself. Try to "act" as if you were depressed now and see how your body changes. Then, get up and move around the way you would if you felt that way. Chances are you're not strutting around with your head up, shoulders back and a grin on your face are you?

Now, the really cool bit about all this technical stuff is that it's widely accepted that because you adopt similar physical positions and movements each time you're having these feelings, the two (the physical position/movement and the feelings) become closely interwoven. You can actually experience some of the feelings and behaviours of being in the states just by adopting the physical positions or movements. (How did you feel acting depressed by the way?)

So, if you want to feel super confident and outgoing on stage, one way is simply to act as if you feel it. To fake it 'til you make it.

Think about a time when you were feeling on top of the world, like you could accomplish anything. Perhaps there was a time when you were on stage and everything was going really well, the audience lapping it all up. Or, if you haven't gigged, maybe your feelings of real confidence and power are more regularly achieved in other fields, business or your personal life for example?

Sit, then stand and move about as you would when you were having those feelings. Now you know how to re-create these positive feelings when you need them.

Here's another trick you can get into the habit of doing to give your self-confidence a boost as soon as you arrive at the venue for the sound check. Try this:

Move some of the furniture around in the room.
We're not talking about re-arranging every table and chair. Just something to psychologically "stamp your authority" on the place. Just a table a couple of inches in one direction or a couple of chairs. Something small. You can even check it's ok with the management to move the object in question (make sure there's some logic to why you'd want to do it). You might be very surprised with the mental boost this can give you.

3.4   <u>Your alter-ego</u>

Sometimes it can be hard to mentally free yourself up to act the way you'd like to do on stage. Perhaps you feel you're just not the out-going or fun-loving person you think you need to be to put on something of a show. Maybe you feel a bit self-conscious.

NLP uses the concept of an alter-ego here. You simply think of someone you admire on stage, someone who behaves the way you'd like to.

You won't be alone when you create your alter-ego. You may have heard of some world famous musicians and performers who use the same technique.

Personally, I thought of two people when I was using this technique and I kind of fused their behaviour into one and gave the resulting "mutation" a name (in private, I'm telling no-one!).

All you do then is to ask yourself how your alter-ego would behave tonight at the gig and then "step into their shoes", become them for the night. It's like putting on a new outfit. The result is that you can break through any mental block about performing.

You don't have to behave in ways which just aren't you on stage. You simply allow yourself, give yourself permission, to *act out the part* you'd like to – just like an actor would, for a couple of hours. You can then revert to being yourself again.

3.5   <u>Don't take yourself too seriously</u>

Here's another trick you can use to immediately put yourself into a relaxed frame of mind just before you go on stage. It's one small action you can take which makes you unable to take yourself too seriously. Mad as I'm sure it sounds, I like to get myself in front of a mirror moments before I go on stage. I wait until I'm alone (in the gents or nip back to the van or car) and then quickly contort a couple of the most insane faces I can imagine at myself. If you're like the other people I've taught this to, and you're doing it right, you'll usually come close to crying with laughter. Try it. Then go out onto the stage and see how difficult it is to feel tense...

3.6   <u>Visualisation and Affirmation</u>

Whether we realise it or not, we're all guilty of imagining the worst is going to happen in certain situations. This can be something simple like momentarily imagining the problems that might arise at the gig, or a little silent voice inside your head casting doubts about your ability.

Visualisation and *affirmation* are two fancy-sounding, but actually very simple, ways of tackling those issues and reducing any impact your own negative thinking might have on you.

You've probably even used them before without knowing it.

With *visualisation* you would simply make yourself think about exactly what the perfect gig would be like. Don't get visualisation mixed up with *wishing* or *hoping*. Visualisation is thinking about the event as if it has *already happened.*

Think about precisely how your audience would react.

What would people come up to you after the gig and say?

How would you feel while playing at this perfect gig?

The key here is to do this thinking or imagining while you're relaxed. So good places for this would be in bed before you go off to sleep or when you first wake up. Any time when you're feeling calm and chilled.

The more detail you can add to this scene, the better the technique will work for you. You don't need to be obsessive about it, to do it over and over. But, if you have a gig coming up that you're anxious about, start to imagine it going your way maybe a week before and then think about it again a few nights before the gig itself.

Generally, the further away the gig is when you start to visualise it, the calmer you'll feel when you run through it in your mind.

Here's a further tip: If you do find yourself tensing up when you think about the forthcoming gig, focus on the *post-gig* period rather than the playing itself. You might, for example, imagine hearing people you know tell you how good the show was, feel them shaking your hand or slapping your back.

Where visualisation is about substituting your unplanned mental pictures and images with ones of your choosing, **affirmation** is about doing the same with words.

In my experience the most effective way to use it is as follows:

31

(i) Think about the most negative thoughts you ever have about yourself and your band as performers. Don't hold back.

(ii) Write these thoughts down on paper as statements. Go for at least 10 different negative statements if you can. For example you might have; *"I'm boring to look at when I play"* or *"We look to old/young/ugly"*, *"we're not great musicians"* or whatever.

(iii) Invert these statements. Think about what the exact opposite statement would be to each of them. So, *"I'm boring to look at when I play"* might become something like; *"I'm exciting to watch whenever I'm playing my drums. People love me and can't take their eyes off me"*.

Don't worry about the fact that this probably isn't true yet or if you feel crazy doing it. No-one will know that you're doing this unless you choose to tell them. Just remember why you're doing this. To rouse your crowds, to give people who watch your band a better time and to enjoy your gigs more yourself. This is for everyone's benefit...

(iv) Ideally, if you can, record yourself speaking these new positive statements (your *"affirmations"*) onto something you can play back at your leisure whenever you're free to do so.

I've used affirmations for years and currently have ones relating to business and music on both my MP3 player for use in the gym, or train and a CD for use on car journeys.

The beauty of both affirmations and visualisation is that these techniques, over time, replace useless negative thoughts you're already having, with positive versions which will help you achieve your goals. They're both free and easy so why wouldn't you be using them?

You'll be able to make these techniques work well to develop sufficient confidence for you with what I've talked through here. However, if you really want to study any of them in more detail, you'll find some books suggested in "Recommended Reading" at the back of the manual.

Now we've looked at the major factors that can get in the way of being focused on audience interaction and how to overcome them. When you no longer need to spend too much time worrying about your playing or singing and you've built your confidence, you'll need to know **how** you're going to engage your crowd and develop real stage presence.

The first place to start is with your set list...

Step 4: Your crowd-rousing plan – Start with your set list

You can make your audience interaction an afterthought; try to slot it in where you can to an existing set list, or you can plan it in as a key part of the gig right from the start; build your sets around involving your audience.

4.1 Doing the hard work in advance

When we first started trying to stir up our audiences, we took our existing set list and worked out what we could do in certain parts of it. For example, there were a couple of numbers that worked well with a member of the audience up on stage with us. These parts of the show were always winners with the crowd so we decided we needed to consciously decide where in the show these songs would work best. We took the interactive moments and songs that involved them and they became the foundations of the show. The rest of the sets were built around them.

Generally speaking, the real highlights should be in the second or final set. This is when the audience will, more often than not, have had a couple of drinks and be more opened up to letting themselves go. You'll probably want to put the bulk of your direct, one-on-one interaction in there.

However, you do need to get something going in the first set to initially hook those assembled in front of you. If you don't, you'll run the risk of large numbers of them leaving (unless it's a private party where generally you're safe no matter how bad you are or how much you ignore / mistreat the crowd).

4.2   <u>Caution! – Dead space ahead</u>

In addition to inserting the greatest highlights of your interaction in your final set and build to a climax at the end, you'll need to work out how to best deal with known dead spaces. Work out where to "place" these throughout the set. As mentioned, dead space can come from guitar changes or tuning etc.

Anticipation is the key to dealing successfully with these known potential trouble spots and using them for some crowd interaction is ideal.

The next page shows an example of a set list from a rock / pop covers gig so you can get the idea of the types of songs and where they've been put in each set. The known dead spaces are highlighted in bold (as they would be on each band member's copy on the night to remind them).

I've italicised the reasons for these dead spaces in brackets after each occasion. Bear in mind the following:

Each change will usually create two potential dead spaces. One for the change itself and another to change back – except if no change back is needed before the end of the set, as in *Twist n Shout* in Set 2.

Set 1

1. Gimme All Your Lovin
2. Cigarettes & Alcohol
3. **Everything's Changing** *(Guitar Change)*
4. Pretty Woman
5. What Difference Does It Make?
6. **Losing My Religion** *(Guitar change back)*
7. **Lithium** *(Tune down)*
8. **Take Me Out** *(Tune back)*
9. American Idiot
10. Should I Stay Or Should I Go?

Set 2

1. Jean Genie
2. Alright Now
3. **You Really Got Me** *(Guitar Change)*
4. Delilah
5. **Sit Down** *(Guitar Change back)*
6. I Want To Break Free
7. **Twist n Shout** *(Guitar Change)*
8. Everyday I Love You Less And Less
9. Somebody Told Me
10. Vertigo

Encore

1. Chasing Cars
2. Whole Lotta Rosie

Guitar changes may not be relevant to you but the principals are the same no matter what the "gaps". To this list of potential "trouble spots" you'll eventually add your ideas for what could be said or done at these times.

As well as "unavoidable" dead space with guitar changes etc, there can also be pregnant pauses between numbers whilst whoever is supposed to kick the next number off waits for everyone else to be ready. This can look and sound very unprofessional and is a big problem for many less experienced bands. Make sure you don't let unplanned gaps in playing lose the momentum you're creating.

More on this later.

4.3   Songs in blocks

Elsewhere in this manual you'll hear mention of song blocks, where bands put two, three or four numbers together and play them without interruption. This is one way to overcome long-winded and unnecessary gaps in between songs, especially if you don't have anything to say.

Some bands or solo artists don't go as far as to string a group of songs together but will try to play two songs without a pause a couple of times in the set. This can be done as simply as the drummer hitting a four count as soon as the last note of the previous song sounds, for example. You can also have some numbers started by another instrument alone and so can be brought straight in if necessary. This way you're eliminating any potentially embarrassing silences.

In the two sets on the previous page, at least half are started by one instrument alone and what they play could expand into double or treble the numbers of bars on the original recording as fills if needed. This is additional insurance against unwanted delays or silences.

4.4   **Don't clear that dance floor**

There are times when you'll want to change the mood by playing something slower during the course of the night. Generally, these will work best early in the night or at your encore / close of the show. Leading your audience into big changes in song style or tempo is a good time for some interaction.

Bear in mind when you're building the set list that you don't want to clear the dance floor or stop the crowd bouncing if you've already managed to get them to that state. The idea is to try and build to a climax with each set. Especially the final set.

Now, with the set list as our basis for audience interaction, let's look at the specific elements that make up **how** to engage the crowd.

PART 2: When you're on stage – Crowd Rousing

5. Even *your* body can get them going

6. Whip up the crowd with your words

7. Look who's talking – Why you don't need a FRONT man (or woman)

8. How to easily spot & seduce really receptive crowd members

9. Timing is everything – The best moments to rouse the crowd at any gig

10. Words to wake up any crowd – Proven stage talk for bands

Step 5: **Even *your* body can get them going**

To start with, we're going to look at the "non-verbal" side of interaction. The communicating you already do even if you don't say a word on stage. The language your body talks: The way you look and move.

Allan Pease is one of the world's foremost experts on the subject of "Body Language". He's sold more than 10 million books across 48 countries so he's someone worth listening to about how to communicate without words.

In his book *"Body Language"* he talks about the importance of your body (rather than just your words alone) in communicating, interacting and the impression you leave on others as a result.

He says:

> *"The total impact of a message is c. 7% verbal (words only), 38% vocal (including the tone of voice, emphasis etc) and 55% non-verbal"*

5.1 **Creating an atmosphere**

Before we get onto what to do with our bodies as a result of knowing this information, it's worth a moment to consider what we can do with the look of the stage area itself.

There are some bands who wouldn't consider gigging

without their expensive lights, fog machines and strobes to give visual impact to their shows. These can all add to an atmosphere for sure. The right lights can work well to set the mood, letting people know something special is about to happen.

Other businesses, restaurants and shops, for example, go to great lengths and expense to establish an ambience and help create positive feelings in their customers. They wouldn't do this if it didn't pay them.

A sound-to-light element to your act can also enhance the rhythm and encourage people to get up and dance. So, if the kinds of places you're playing don't have their own lights, you might want to consider this.

You can get a decent set of basic lights for around £100 from places like Maplins and significantly less off EBay.

However, some places you'll play may be too small for this kind of additional gear or they'll be large enough to have their own lights. Other times you just won't want to be bothered carrying lights. In any case, just like a rich kid with a 70's series Strat who can only play 3 chords – no amount of gear will save you if you don't know what you're supposed to be doing – in this case putting on a show.

5.2   **Body Talk**

Knowing what words to say to your crowd in those awkward moments is something that makes many front men or women and other band members nervous. But consider Allan Pease's statement again:

> *"The total impact of a message is c. 7% verbal (words only), 38% vocal (including the tone of voice, emphasis etc) and 55% non-verbal"*

The bulk of the impact of your message, the impression you leave on people in any situation, will not come from (the content of) your words. In fact, people will get a bigger impression simply from the **way** you say your words rather than what those words actually are.

As musicians we're obviously concerned with sound but the knowledge that so much of your impact can come from the way you look and move is a very powerful fact. Once you accept the concept and learn how to use the information, it can give a great confidence boost to your performances.

The impact your look and movement have is one reason why the top pro bands don't really have to say a great deal on stage to go down brilliantly. Their reputation and videos have done a lot of the work for them before they even set foot in front of their congregations.

You probably don't yet have this luxury. So you have to work on your body language. First, to make sure that it's saying what you want and second that it's understood by your audience.

Here are a few simple rules to follow to get you started.

5.3   **Amplification is NOT just about your sound**

The first thing to remember about performing on the stage, or even if you're just singing in a corner of a bar or coffee shop, is *to "amplify"* your look and movements in a way that will engage onlookers.

Most people won't be able to see you as closely as they would in a one-to-one situation. Every movement, gesture or facial expression will need to be bigger and bolder if you want it to be seen. What you wear may need to be more exaggerated than would normally be the case. You don't need a fancy dress costume, just something that makes you stand out more than you would in the street. How about some accessories? A hat or jewellery for example. There's plenty you can do, even if you don't want to look like The Edge, Flavor Flav or generally unhinged.

But what are you going to do with your body once it's "dressed"?

5.4   When you're smiling

It won't surprise you to know that smiling is not a natural response to feeling frightened or nervous on stage. Nor is it the first thing that comes to mind when you think you need to look cool. Also, when a musician is so into his music that he forgets about his audience, he's unlikely to be grinning.

Simple and cheesy as it may sound, smiling on stage will do much to warm your audience to you. Smiling shows you remember the people watching and you're warm to them. It allows them to remember you're human (after all). It can convey the "fact" you're down to earth and approachable. These are useful traits if you want people to come over and ask about booking you for private parties and events for example.

Looking moody and not smiling might look hot to some people and it may do no harm to have one or two of you looking that way. But, do you want the whole band to frown their way through 2 or 3 sets? How is that likely to make people in the crowd feel about you when they've never seen you before?

Many musicians have to hold their hands up here and admit that early video evidence confirms them guilty as serial offenders. Not necessarily cool but certainly frowning.

Smiling from time to time when you're playing came back as one of the key recommendations for generating positive crowd response through the research I did with other performing musicians.

One other good reason for remembering to smile; if you think back to what we spoke about in *"Fake it 'til you make it"* in Step 3.3, you'll remember how any emotion or feeling you have has a physical action connected to it. So, smiling when you initially don't feel like it can help you feel like you would if you really wanted to smile...

A good enough reason to start smiling I'd say anyhow.

So, one person at least (maybe whoever is going to be responsible for most interaction) make sure you pick people or groups of people out in the crowd and smile at them regularly throughout the gig. Later we'll look at the best potential targets for your toothy (or toothless) grins.

5.5 <u>The eyes have it</u>

Author *Eckhard Hess* dedicated his life to the study of

'Pupillometrics'. This measures the eyes' responses to viewed objects and people. In his book "*The Tell Tale Eye*: *How Your Eyes Reveal Hidden Thoughts and Emotions*" he says:

> "*The eyes ...give the most revealing and accurate of all human communication signals because they are the focal point on the body.*"

We all know that some people make us feel comfortable when they're in front of us while others leave us feeling uneasy. Studies have shown that this has much to do with the length of time they look at us or hold our gaze as they speak.

What does this mean for you the musician?

It's quite simple really: *Make eye contact with the crowd.*

Shy and introverted people don't generally make eye contact as a rule. You might not be a natural extrovert but here are three tips that can help you to break this pattern.

a) Ask yourself "*what colour are their eyes?*" each time you look at someone. If it's dark in the crowd just try to tell whether the eyes are light (green or blue) or dark (brown). This will force you to make at least initial eye contact with people.

b) Imagine there are strings connecting your eyes to those of the people you choose to look at in the crowd. This will keep you connected to them.

c) If you're not making actual eye contact with individuals (perhaps because it's a dark room with a lot of people), you can aim to put your gaze on a spot on the far wall of the room. This way you'll give the impression of making eye contact with the crowd.

5.6   <u>Open up</u>

Another important element in the impression you make on others when you perform is your openness.

Throughout history, displays of "physical openness" have generally been considered to indicate three things about a person:

(i)   That the person is honest
(ii)   feeling positive towards you and
(iii)   is non-threatening.

This "open" body language can be something like not folding our arms when talking face to face to others for example.   How positive do you feel if you approach someone you like the look of and they fold their arms when you speak?

Salespeople, who's livelihoods depend on getting on with others (or at least making others suspend any negative thoughts about them long enough for them to sell them something), are taught to open up the palms of their hands when trying to convince other people of what they're saying and selling. They're also told to keep their hands away from their own faces when in front of others – i.e. not to put barriers up in front of their faces but rather to keep them 'opened up'.

What use can this knowledge be to us gigging musicians?

You should try to be conscious of any barriers between you and the crowd.

Think of the pro singer, who occasionally takes his mic from the stand and moves the stand to the side, from directly in-between themselves and the audience.

Guitarists can do something to open up as well. Low slung guitars aren't only for trying to look cool. A lowered guitar position shows off more of your upper body and so reduces the barrier between you and the audience.

But playing a low guitar right through a show won't suit every guitarist. Instead you could tilt the head of the guitar down at times in between songs to show more of yourself, even move the guitar around towards your back.

If your lead singer also plays guitar, could you do without his or her strumming on a couple of numbers? Without their guitar in front of them for a while they would be more "opened up" to the crowd.

Clearly, "opening up" may be more difficult for a keyboard player or drummer but, as you'll see, there are ways these guys can get out from behind their gear as well.

Just keep in mind that you're trying to minimise any barriers to intimacy or connection between you and your audience at times while you're playing.

5.7   I like the way you move

One of the most uncomfortable sights many bands ever see is the videos of their early performances. Seeing just how stationary they are on stage can be very uninspiring. And of course, the audience are usually pretty much the same. Who could blame them?

How can any band expect to move their audience, to give their audience a good time when they're not moving themselves or they look bored / scared to be playing?

As Carly, a keyboard player member of a band from Boston in the U.S. put it:

> *"Energy and enthusiasm are infectious, and I plan on infecting as many people as I can."*

This is where a study of your favourite live bands will come in useful. You can watch their antics (on YouTube if you can't afford the gig) and then adapt what they do. Just give yourself ideas.

A semi-pro guitarist in the States, who's generally thought of as a great mover when he's on stage, told of how he actually studied dancers both in clubs and watching videos online. These people he studied weren't other musicians, just dancers. He'd then get himself in front of the mirror at home and adapt some of the best moves into something he could do with a guitar around his neck.

Like I said, this guy is now thought to have a great "stage presence" but he himself admitted there was a time when he was, as he put it, a *"Stereo-typical white boy – no rhythm"*.

He went on to say that if it worked for him it can work for anyone.

Keep in mind what we discussed in 5.3. Namely that any gestures or movements on stage need to be amplified to communicate across the distance (no matter how short) to the watching crowd.

So, remember to exaggerate any movements you make on stage for maximum effect – and, like we saw in Step 1, practise in front of mirrors and videos until you're happy with what you see.

Once we've got the moves, we need to ask ourselves how are we going to **talk** to our crowds?

Step 6: **Whip up the crowd with your words**

6.1 <u>Walking the fine line</u>

Planning some of what and when you're going to say things to the crowd will help you avoid any problems caused by the following fact:

There's a fine line between you talking too little and too much to the crowd at your gigs.

Recording your rehearsals (where you practise your stage talk) or your gigs once you're putting your planning into practise, will help you get the balance you need between too much and too little talk.

6.2 <u>It's the *way you* tell them</u>

When you start to think about what you're going to say to the crowd, keep in mind what you learnt from Step 5.

Namely, that as far as your communication is concerned, less than 10% of the impact you make will be as a result of the words you use.

The bulk of the impression you make will come from the *way* you talk and the way you *look* when you're saying it.

What does this mean?

It means you should think not only about the *words* you're going to use in anything you say to the crowd but, much more importantly, *how* you say these words.

So, deliver what you say using the tips you learnt about body language in the last step. Remember, you can always fake confidence and even friendliness until you really feel them if you need to by smiling, eye contact and your posture.

Now here are some talking tips to help with your **delivery**, that all-important largest element of your verbal message.

6.3   **What did she say?**

To paraphrase Steve Cohen in his inspiring book *"Win the crowd"*:

> *"You cannot connect with a crowd if they can't hear you properly and they're constantly asking each other what you just said."*

So, you need to speak up and out when you talk to the crowd.

Here are two pointers which help:

- *Aim you words out towards the top of the far wall in the room.*
This will ensure you project them far enough to avoid mumbling.

- *Deliberately talk louder than feels natural to you.*
This is the essence of raising your voice. If the volume you're talking at on stage doesn't feel raised to you in any way, then it's not going to be loud enough. If in doubt, imagine a little old groupie at the very back of the room who wants to hear every word you say and project yourself so they will be in no doubt.

6.4 Slow and easy

When we're excited and/or nervous, we have a tendency to rush our words when we speak. It's almost as if we want to get the words out of the way. Similar, in some ways, to a person speaking too quietly to be heard properly when they're shy.

Someone talking quickly can be difficult to understand and if an audience has to struggle to understand what you're saying they're likely to give up and switch off. Or maybe just shout:

> *"Get on with it!"*

- Obviously not great for anyone's confidence.

So, try to consciously talk more slowly than you normally would when you're on stage. If it feels you're talking at your normal pace then you're going too fast.

Volume and speed of speech are in some ways connected so you should find these improvements will work together as you put them into practise.

6.5 <u>Mic technique</u>

A common mistake amateur and semi-pro performers make is talking (and singing) with the microphone too far from their mouths.

The result with poor mic technique like this is that your talking (and of course singing) will sound muffled and distorted or too distant / quiet.

Many times you can get away with this when you're singing, especially if you're only backing vocals. But when we talk we're less likely to belt the words out. So, if you have lousy mic technique this will really show up when you do talk and make it difficult to understand you.

To prevent this, just make sure you get up very close to the mic when you talk, ideally with some compression for the voice if you have it.

Another thing to remember here is about any effects you may have on your voice. If you have a lot of reverb on your voice for example, make sure you know the impact it has on your speaking voice. You'll probably want to mute it when you come to talk or the audience won't appreciate your pearls of wisdom.

So, the building blocks of being able to whip up the crowd with your words are:

(i)   Speak up
(ii)   Speak out
(iii) Talk more slowly than you normally would.
(iv)   Watch how you use your mic

This will make sure you're heard and understood.

The next step to look at is **who** in your band (assuming you're not a solo performer in which case you'll know the answer), will do the on stage banter...

Whip up the crowd with your words

Step 7: Look who's talking – Why you don't need a FRONT man (or woman)

As a band, you'll want to think about your look as a whole and also about what, if anything, each of you is going to do about some form of stage presence. About contributing as a "whole" to the band's total stage persona.

Typically it's the front man or woman, the one who does most of the singing, who's the focal point in a band situation. If yours is someone who enjoys being in the spotlight then maybe you'll allow him or her to be responsible for almost all the interaction. Sometimes that will suit the whole band.

Sometimes though, even when there's one out and out extrovert who maybe happens to be the front man, there are others who want to share the spotlight.

7.1 Who wants to be involved?

If you're not a solo artist then the first step is to see who in the band actively wants to be involved in your audience interaction.

You may have one or more band members who feel too uncomfortable to approach the mic or move on stage. If you do, but you're convinced these members contribute to the band enough musically or in other ways, whoever's willing is going to have to be big enough to take on the responsibility for the "show" themselves.

No problem if those include an outgoing lead singer. If not though, you'll have to get a little more creative about what you do and design the interactive elements of your show around those band mates who are prepared to be involved.

If your lead singer or front person doesn't feel comfortable engaging the crowd, you can in fact make it work as a unique feature for your band. However, do try to get them to at least say *"thanks"* after some of the songs.

You'll probably find that, like many musicians, once you do get involved in some responsive audience banter, even if you're the very shyest type of band member, your confidence grows. You'll want more of the buzz that feeding off the crowd can give you.

Keep in mind that things change and those who want to be involved in the interaction (and to what extent) can alter over time. Where you start from in terms of your crowd interaction is likely to be very different from the way you perform a year or two down the line.

Also, think about how it may look to an audience if only one person is interacting with the crowd. Like it or not, it will seem that he or she is the "leader". So if you're not happy with that you better get more involved!

7.2 **All quiet at the back?**

Any band member can contribute to your audience interaction. If the extrovert in the band is your drummer, there's still plenty you can do to use this quality to spice up your shows.

- Move them from the traditional drummer's spot at the back. Seat them to the side of the stage facing across the rest of the band – or even at the front.

- Buy (or build) a portable, collapsible drum riser if the size of your typical gig venue will permit.

Either way, your drummer will be more exposed to the crowd, closer to the front of the stage and encouraged more to put on a show. Also, if they're the one doing a lot of the between-song chat, it makes more sense if the audience can see them.

There are things beyond their on stage position which you can do to play to the strength of an extrovert drummer and get them in your audience focus:

- For the odd big finish or two, where they can do without the bass pedals, have them get off their seat and walk around their kit smashing the cymbals or toms. They can then be back in their seat for the final chord slam.

- If they can sing, let them handle vocals for at least one track. If you haven't moved them from the back, give them a name-check before the song and even have them stand up and wave to the crowd before they start. Most people won't get much of a look at the drummer throughout the gig, hidden as most skin-beaters will be, behind their kits. This move almost always gets a big reaction.

- Get the drummer to lower their cymbals – or remove

any they don't need. This will give the crowd a better chance of seeing them. (If, however, they're not contributing to audience engagement and aren't great to look at, you might want to consider asking them to buy more cymbals).

- Get some lights and light the drummer up! If you're using stage lights just make sure they're not shrouded in darkness there at the back. If you position at least one of the lights behind them (though not close enough to overheat/burn) they should shine through the kit, lighting the drummer and the kit up as well as the stage. If you don't have your own stage lights, they can use some clip-on reading lights to make themselves more visible.

- If there's a section of a song without any drums, consider having them move, get up and walk around the stage. Can they dance?

- Accessorise the drummer. An over the top hat or glasses can add some mystique to even the dullest looking individual.

If a drummer can get involved in rousing your crowds, ultimately, any band member can and probably should be involved in the "show" side of your gig. The ideas above should get you thinking about how this can work with guitarists, keyboard players or other musicians.

The very least every band member should be doing is looking like they're into the music and enjoying themselves. Even that will encourage the crowd to have a good time. Isn't that what it's all about?

7.3 **Who's going to do what?**

In a band situation, once you've sorted out who wants to be involved, you need to think about who does what. If you don't, you risk a free-for–all every time there's a lull in between songs when everyone steps forward to their mic.

Go back to your set list again as a point of reference to plan from.

If you've planned your set list out to minimise dead space and thought about where and possibly what kind of things you want to say, it becomes a relatively easy thing to apportion out who takes responsibility for which bit.

Maybe one person will handle the bulk of what talking there is but others might introduce a couple of songs each, handle the band member introductions (if you do them), mention the next appearance at the venue or point the crowd to your website or merchandise.

You have to formally agree exactly who's going to do what. Some parts can remain fluid so that if someone thinks of something to say at any point they're free to come out with it. But they can do this in the knowledge of who and what they have to slot their words or actions in and around. There should be certain places where, if one person has previously "claimed" it for some interaction, that claim is respected.

Now you know that anyone in a band can play their part in your audience interaction and you've got some ideas on how they could start to go about this. Let's look at *which members of the audience* you should direct your words, actions and blossoming stage presence towards.

Look who's talking – Why you don't need a FRONT man (or woman)

Step 8: How to easily spot & seduce really receptive crowd members

As you stand up there in what can feel like a lonely spot on stage, it's tempting to think of those people watching you (no matter how few there are) as all being the same.

This is a mistake and here's why:

8.1 Not all crowd members are created equal

If you think about it, in any gig crowd on any night there are a number of reasons people could be there watching:

- Some may have seen you before and want to watch you again
- Others are compulsive band watchers and come out for whoever's playing the venue
- Some are musicians out to check on the competition (if they're studying your fret work with head cocked to one side and a smug facial expression, you can be sure)
- Some may have stumbled into the place for a good time
- If the place serves food, some people may have come to eat and just still be there having a drink afterwards (i.e. they don't care whether there's a band on or not).

These different reasons can be the cause of different types

of behaviour within any crowd and this is something you can use to build your night.

8.2 Seek out your "helpers" early on

This is probably the most valuable tip many bands ever discover about audience interaction. To really engage a crowd you don't just put out your best moves or one-liners and hope someone responds.

You should, from very early on, actively seek out the best candidates to use your moves and words on. Even just to use the bulk of your smiles and eye contact with.

The reason you do this will become clear shortly.

If the gig is a private party for example, then the birthday boy or bride and groom, best man, bridesmaids or whoever are obvious targets. What if it's a public gig though? How do you identify the people who will help you with your show?

Steve Cohen again in *"Win the Crowd"* is looking for what he calls the *"key people"* in the crowd with the widest (most "dilated") eye pupils. He does this because eyes dilate when someone is looking at something that interests or excites them.

But Steve's a table magician – albeit an extremely wealthy and successful one, and he sees his crowd at close quarters.

Now, unless your gig is a pretty intimate (or possibly even cramped) affair, you probably aren't going to be able to see many people's pupils. Possibly those at the very front – who may or may not seem to be into the band.

At any gig though, there will be people who are more open and responsive to the band. You need to check out the room early on, as soon as you start playing. It can even pay to check the room out a little while you're setting up and shortly before you go on stage.

See who looks like they're having a good time, maybe had a few drinks (although make sure they don't look likely to have overdone it and be spoiling for a fight). Look for those who seem most up for a good time. They'll be moving a little more than most when you start playing, singing along or just looking intently at one of the band. If you're lucky they might even be dancing.

Try to find a number of these people or groups scattered around the room. Even when there's only one, that can still be enough to work the magic you need.

You can smile at them and say hello or a few words before the show if you spot them early enough and feel like talking to them.

Keep in mind that once these helpers are identified, you have to make sure you don't ignore other people during the show.

Now, the beauty of playing up to these people and encouraging them to be even more extroverted is that, in doing so, you'll actually encourage the rest of the crowd to have a better time. It seems to give other people "permission" to open up and go for it a little more themselves.

Try it and you'll see what I mean.

8.3 <u>Get into them - Go wireless</u>

An ideal way to check out who seems most up for it is by going wireless. You don't (necessarily) need the whole band roaming. Just one person will do. Provided they don't mind getting out front early on and having a look around. They may need some extra confidence to do this so see some of the points in Step 3 for ideas.

By going wireless you can check every corner of the room in case there are people getting on down in remote areas. Get up real close and you can even make like a table magician and check the crowd's pupils if it's not too dark.

Most musicians (myself included) who play wireless wouldn't have it any other way. When they feel like it, they can get out there and make a clown of themselves. The audience members who don't want to get involved (generally through embarrassment) will make themselves as obvious as those who do.

Those who are up for it will look at you and start bopping along all the more. Smile at them and go over to them throwing a few overdone moves or facial expressions as you do.

Some crowd members suspect you can't actually be playing if you're wandering around so far from the stage. You might want to let them pluck the odd string while you hold the chord down.

What's cool about going wireless, is that getting into the crowd is the same as getting an audience member up on stage; it breaks down any barriers that exist between band and crowd. It stops them and you being strangers to each other.

I know singers who go wireless and will wander around shaking a tambourine, creep up behind people at the bar or jump up and start dancing on tables. Mostly over the top, but if you're up for it you can rest assured there'll be members of the audience who'll love it.

Go out & Pick people to play

There's one other particularly good reason for wandering around wireless. You can "scout" for likely candidates for later when you may want to get someone up on stage with you.

8.4   Audience participation – get them up

I promise you this, if you can get a member or two of the audience up and onto the stage, it will do more than anything else you could do to make for a memorable night for everyone.

Those who do get up onto the stage will only be those who want to be there, even if they play at being reluctantly in the spotlight. Everyone else watching will identify with the person up on stage. Some will be relieved that they're now under no pressure to get up there. Others will be keenly waiting for the next opportunity so that they can get up there themselves.

Playing Simple instruments.

As far as the band is concerned, you're the ones in control so it will pay you to get someone up that your audience will enjoy watching for whatever reason.

You're obviously free to use your discretion and only invite up someone you'd like to see a little closer or maybe get to know a little better if that suits you and you're not too creepy about it.

How do you get people to join you in front of everyone else?

As we said earlier, if it's a private party, you get the host or birthday boy/wedding couple up, more than once if necessary. Congratulate them and let people acknowledge them. If it's a public gig, the easiest way, as you'll see in Step 10, is to tell them you:

> *"Need some help on stage."*

This "help" can take the form of some additional rhythm (pack a spare tambourine, bongo drums or triangle – yes really), backing vocals & dancing (see above), you can get someone up to be *"sung to"*, an *"air guitar contest"* or to interact with inflatables or other props.

More on this later.

When you really engage audiences like this they'll be queuing up to get on there. Just make sure you don't invite anyone so drunk they crash into your gear. I've seen this happen and the bloody aftermath. Believe me – it ain't pretty.

8.5 A word of warning on who to invite on stage

When you invite someone up onto the stage, check out who they're with first.

Here's a cautionary tale from a middle-aged weekend warrior who was playing bass in Bolton, England.

One night, during a less than taxing number, he went walkabout with his wireless pack. There was an area of the bar the band couldn't see from the stage and a group of people around that corner were really getting off on the song.

He motioned for one of the ladies to follow him from their table, which she did. They ended up on the dance floor together jigging around a little. Because she knew all the song words and was singing along loudly, he suggested she get up on the stage and use his mic to do some backing vocals.

This is generally only a risk in terms of the kind of noise they might make or them being too drunk to stand and collapsing into your gear as mentioned earlier.

Once she was up there, the bassist went back to her table to tell her companions to check her out on the stage. It was then that he saw who she was with. Muscle-bound, tattooed and, by the sour look in his eyes, none too happy. Above the music the bass player tried to say:

"You didn't mind me inviting her to join us did you?"

Eventually muscles cracked a smile and said it was fine. Let this show you to at least pay attention to who a person is with before you invite them up. If in doubt, try a wink or smile at their partner before you approach the person in question.

8.6 **Bring your own "key people"**

If you don't want to leave anything to chance and you have friends who'll be at the gig, they can be used as back up *"show assistants"* or *"fire starters"*, call them what you will. They can be useful in getting some action going between you and the crowd.

The thing is to have someone who seems to be having a great time watching the band. This, as I mentioned earlier, sort of gives everyone else "permission" to let themselves go more.

Every time you play, keep in mind not all crowd members are the same.

Focus on finding those few key people who will help you out during the show. At the same time be careful not to totally ignore everyone else.

Once you have these leading players identified you need to know the best, most effective moments during the show to engage them.

Let's look at these now.

Step 9: **Timing is everything – The best moments to rouse the crowd at any gig**

Working from the set list you've put together, these are key moments which are ideal opportunities for you to consciously engage your crowd:

- At the show (or set) opening
- In between songs
- During any dead space due to guitar tunings or technical problems
- Audience requests
- Changes in song style or tempo
- Band member introductions
- In between the sets (i.e., when you're OFF stage)
- Audience participation
- Hecklers

Let me talk you through each of these individually.

9.1 **Show or set opening**

Some bands like to rip straight into their first number without so much as a *"Hello Southend!"* That's fine and you should work out your own style. However, if you don't at some point acknowledge the crowd fairly early on, you'll leave that barrier up which will get harder to break down the longer the night goes on.

There are three main approaches here:

73

- You can say hello before you play a note then dive into the playing.

- Leave it until after the first song, so that the number has done the groundwork.

- The final approach is to play through the first group of songs (say three numbers), without any pause between them.

  You start the second immediately after the first has finished etc. Then, after tension has mounted a little, you grant your audience a reprieve and pause after a maximum of three numbers to get the intros out of the way and engage the crowd.

Any of these will work and you should experiment to see which best suits your act. The beauty is that, like most of the techniques discussed throughout this manual, you can rotate them when you're at a repeat venue to keep yourself looking and sounding "fresh" to what may be a lot of the same people each time.

9.2   **In between songs**

If you've written the song you're about to sing, you can talk a little about what inspired it. That lost love or great car you used to own. This can give you a chance to open up a little to the audience, let them feel they're getting to know you a bit.

If it's a cover and a natural place to talk, you can say something interesting, relevant, funny and brief about the artists or writer. Do a little research.

Or, using the same intention as if you wrote the song, talk about why it means something to you or one of the band.

Another way to talk about the forthcoming song, and which you can use to alternate with what the number means to you, is to look for potential relevance with audience members and ask simple questions like:

> *"Anyone here into the Kaiser Chiefs?"*

This most basic question about any reasonably well-known band will get some response you'll be able to work with. When you get a shout or groan you can answer with:

> *"Well this is just for you then."*

or:

> *"Not like this you won't!"*

If the next song is one you've written about breaking up with a partner, for example, you can ask:

> *"Anyone else here celebrating divorce or separation?"*

What happens if you don't get a response? In truth on 90% of occasions, as long as the questions aren't too obscure (*"anyone else like Albanian rail journeys?"* etc), you will get some response. But in the unlikely event you don't, a simple:

> *"Ah well, we'll play this anyway, you might like it."*

or:

> *"OK, well we'll play this for everyone who's determined to stay in their relationship no matter what."*

You don't want to talk in between every song. Planning the night with your set list, you can pick and choose your moments and only talk when you have your best ideas of what to say.

9.3   Dead space due to tunings or technical problems

Early in their gigging days, many bands and solo artists are horrified listening back to live recordings with the amount of gaps they were leaving in between each number. Some of these musicians tell me they can't believe the audiences ever stayed in the venue some nights.

If you have this problem you'll need to address it with a little planning.

Take each song and work out how you could start it. Everyone take some responsibility. There will be numbers you could start on bass, others on guitar and of course the usual 4 count on drums. Each individual instrument could play alone for a few bars which will indicate to the other band members that they better get ready to contribute because the song is happening!

This means unnecessary pauses and dead spaces can be all but eliminated.

Everyone will know which songs they are responsible for starting. If memory is not your strong point, you should mark who starts what on your copy of the set list. There will be gaps in between songs which are necessary. If you need to tune a guitar down for a particular number, fit a capo or have technical problems, you're not going to want lengthy pregnant pauses while your audience fidget uncomfortably. Factor into your planning something to say at this point.

You can have your drummer, or whoever's not busy, do a little talking. This is a good way to get all band members involved to some extent and to make them more visible to the audience.

Tim, a lead guitarist and Gig-Getter user from Malta, told me about how, a few years ago, their frontman / 2nd guitarist broke 2 guitar strings in quick succession. After mumbling a couple of things while he was changing his first snap, the rest of the band ran out of things to say. The experience of willing a deep hole in the venue floor to open up and help the band disappear taught them something. They're all now briefed and armed with a plan of action for any eventuality. So should you be.

9.4 Audience requests

If someone comes up to you while you're on stage to ask for a particular song or if you're approached with a request in between sets, these are good opportunities to talk to the crowd. Use the details after they've finished talking to you or when you're back on stage.

There are some ideas of what you can say in Step 10. The point is that when someone makes a request you have a completely valid reason to talk to your crowd and involve them.

9.5 Changes in song style or tempo

This is an ideal time to set the scene for what's to follow. Say you've been hitting it hard with a couple of rock numbers and are about to go into a ballad. You can't really just abruptly stop what you've been doing and slow it all down. You need to let your audience know what's going to happen. Guide them through it.

It needn't be an opportunity for everyone to leave the dance floor. You can say something like:

> *"Ok gents / lads, now's the time to get your better half or any lady up on the dance floor for a slow one."*

Similarly, if you've been doing a few slower numbers, invite people onto the floor now that you're going into an up-tempo number.

9.6 Band member introductions

Always a great way to further break down any barriers between crowd and band and to ensure no-one thinks you're putting yourselves on pedestals. Many musicians I work with firmly believe it also helps encourage people to approach you after the gig to ask about private party work or anything else you might want to tout for.

Generally, band introductions are better left until very near the second / last set. If you try it early on it can be a case of the audience thinking:

> *"So what? Do I even know these people?"*

Wait until you've been through something together, namely the preceding couple of hours.

You might prefer your band to vamp over the introduction, to extend it or play some background stuff rather than have nothing going on under the verbal intros. You can get some ideas of what you might say about each other in Step 10. Usually one person will introduce everyone but themselves. Just make sure you know who'll take over and introduce the main announcer with a *"Last but by no means least..."* intro of his own. The intros can be neatly included at around the same time you say "Goodnight" to your audience.

9.7   In between sets - when you're OFF stage

This is one I've often seen ignored by bands. You don't need to go round trying to get business but it will do you no harm to make sure people realise you are approachable should they want to book you, ask about CDs and merchandise or just chat with you / tell you how great you are etc.

You can also "mingle" with the punters before the gig, in between sets, at the bar and of course while you're packing up providing there are still people in the venue after you've finished. Don't neglect this time to cement relationships and to remind people about the website and merchandise if you're selling it.

Just smile and make eye contact again when you come off. It can be a fine balance between appearing friendly and needy in terms of wanting praise so, like most things, practise makes perfect. You'll know when you get it right because you'll get approaches.

79

9.8   With an audience member up on stage

In Step 8 I suggested getting an audience member or two up on stage with you. If you do this, clearly you'll need to talk to your "guests" at this point.

9.9   Dealing with hecklers

In reality anyone trying to shout abuse at you is very unlikely unless you really aren't rehearsed enough to be gigging or the musical talent of the whole band leaves a lot to be desired.

However, if you do get some drunkard trying to bawl you out, you'll find specific suggestions for how to deal with them in the next step. Alternatively, just make sure you reduce any dead space they might take advantage of and that you're playing is loud enough to drown his or her nonsense out.

9.10   "Thank you...and Goodnight!"

Before the final number you'll want to thank the audience for coming (and staying) and if relevant remind them again about your merchandise, website or, if you know it, your next appearance. You should aim to do this during the set itself with just a simple thanks and goodnight at the end of the encore.

Ok, so we've looked at **when** the most effective times to try to connect with the crowd are. Now you're going to get some specific ideas of exactly **what** you can say at these times.

Step 10:   Words to wake up any crowd - Proven stage talk for bands

So now you're armed with the facts that:

1. The bulk of your crowd communication comes from the *way you look*

2. Next most important is the *way* you say things, not what you say

The previous steps have given you plenty of ideas to improve in both those areas. However, there is also another area in particular where musicians can get very uptight and which I've found is a major cause for concern on gig night. This area is knowing **what** to say when you try to talk to those people in front of you.

So, once you have the way you look and how you're going to talk sorted, you're going to want some ideas about *content*. About what you could and should say to get good reactions and start some audience engagement.

What follows are numerous one-liners and recommendations from either my own experience or which have been used and recommended by other successful semi-pro bands and musicians.

There are 6 categories of things you can say that will give you plenty to talk about when you need it and will have the most impact when you're out there.

These categories are:

- Using props
- Encourage people to drink
- Introduce and thank the bar staff
- Shameless self-promotion
- Talk about the venue, town or region
- Tried & tested sound bites and one-liners to have fun with

10.1 Using props

These can be a great help in giving you something other than yourself or the song or even the audience to talk about. With a **tambourine** for example, you can raise it at a moment of your choosing between songs and say:

> *"Right* (raising and shaking tambourine) *we need some help with our rhythm"*

or:

> *"Anyone got rhythm they'd like to share?"*

Ask for volunteers. If you get none, look to one of the noisier tables identified during the evening and give them a shout or approach them.

When you find someone suitable, you can take their arm or hand to help get them up onto the stage (most people will feel some apprehension and so welcome this reassurance).

As you've been hearing throughout this manual, your audiences will love to see audience participation. If one person refuses to help you, move on to the next person.

Your judgment of who's up for it will improve each time you invite someone up.

Inflatable guitars can be used to hold impromptu air guitar sessions for audience members. Pick two and get them to "axe-off" in front of the stage during a heavier number, ideally with a solo. This works well when one of the chosen is the party host (and so especially game for – or at least feeling obliged to provide a laugh) or has a birthday etc. Use your creativity here and you'll come up with plenty of ideas.

10.2   Encourage people to drink

Remind them of any special offers at the bar and of how much better you sound the more they drink. The venue management will appreciate you trying to boost their takings.

10.3   Introduce & thank the bar staff

The staff will love it if you take the trouble to learn some of their names and give them a name check when you play. You can suggest the crowd tips them when they buy drinks – add *"They look better on their sides"* or such like if you feel the need.   See 10.6 below for more ideas of what you can say.

10.4   Shameless self-promotion

No-one wants to stand on stage bawling out adverts like some carnival barker. However, there are some things that will help your audience out – providing you don't overdo it.

- Merchandise
If you're offering any CDs or T-shirts etc don't be shy in pointing people in the direction of the table you're selling from and giving the name of the person selling for you who can help the audience members out.

- Website
Don't forget to give people details of where you can be found online to encourage them to visit. A good tip here is to take photographs yourselves during the gig (see Gig-Getter manual) and then tell the audience to visit the website after the weekend to see if their picture is on there.

- Next appearance
Mention the next time you're appearing at the venue – if you know it. You can also plug gigs elsewhere in the same area if it's not on a night that competes with the current venue's gig nights and you ok it with the management to mention it first. Point to the website address or contact number on your monitors, banner at the back of the stage or flyers / cards around the room (you do have these printed somewhere don't you?). Tell the audience you can be contacted about private parties etc from there. This is, of course, if you play them and if you want to push yourselves.

10.5 Talk about the venue, town or region

Start with some factor of the immediate location and work out from there. This could be some comment about the stage, the dance floor, room, bar, venue, town, region etc.

When you go through your set list beforehand, see whether there are any connections with where you're playing.

One covers band near Seattle introduces a song that they play by Nirvana as a *"song by a local band"* when they're playing close to home.

If you write your own material, mention any connection one of the band may have to the region or link something in the region into the inspiration for writing the song if it makes sense.

10.6 **Tried & tested sound bites and one-liners to have fun with**

As I've mentioned before, some people might not like the idea of scripted lines to use and feel that every audience is distinctive in their own right.

There's some truth in this but here are four things to remember if you're worried about the idea of a "script".

(i)   A handful of reliable one-liners can be your fallback position if you really can't think of anything to say on the night. You need never be fearful of drying up if you have some prepared ideas with you on gig night.

(ii)   Once your confidence has grown by talking on stage, you can (and should) use your creativity with the following recommendations to adapt and adjust to fit each occasion.

(iii)   In time you'll develop and add your own one-liners and phrases through experience of what works and what doesn't for you. I've left you some space at the end so that you can write them in and keep it all together.

(iv)   If in doubt, be reassured that even some of the greatest artists use "scripted spontaneity". Anyone who's seen their favourite band play more than once on the same tour will have no doubt about this. If it's good enough for millionaire rockers....

Here, then, are some specific ideas for things to say at certain points in a gig. Many of these will show you don't take yourself too seriously. If that isn't the kind of image you want to portray, just pick and choose the ones that suit you or adapt them as you see fit.

All these have been proven to get great reactions by various bands and solo artists around the world.

One final thought. Remember what you learned earlier? It's the *way* you say your words that's most important. Some of these phrases may not appeal on paper but will have a completely different impact when spoken the right way at a gig.

Set/Show Starts

- *"What I do is tell a few jokes, sing a few songs, drink beer, meet women and I get paid. Is this a great job or what?"*

- *"Well..., you're probably all nervous wondering what I'm going to think of you."*

(works for the start of the night's playing or after the first couple of songs)

- *"Welcome to my mid-life crisis."*

- *"We're <u><insert band name here></u>!! We're gonna show you all a good time".*

(Make sure you can follow-up your claims with this one.)

- *"And we'd just like to say, that we don't have any computers up here, and we don't have any synthesizers, and we don't have any special effects that makes it sound like an orchestra is playing. Everything tonight is real, hand-made, strait-up, no bulls**t, honest to God, get down, kick it around, good old fashioned Rock 'n Roll!"*

After 1st Song

- *"Hey where did everybody go?"*

- *"My people..."*   – after applause

- "*Alright. We played <u><insert rival/adjacent town name></u> last night and they made a ton of noise, let's see if you can show them up, make some f***ing noise!!*"

Then, even if they are loud, tell them they can do better and make them scream again. Clearly this will work better for some sorts of music, venues or occasions than others.

- After the first song you can introduce your band as someone else e.g.

   "*Good evening people, for those of you who don't know us, we are Van Halen.*"

- "*THANK YOU!!!...Goodnight everybody! Be careful going home!*"

- "*Don't everyone clap together. You might create a rhythm and confuse the drummer.*"

- Ask the audience:

   "*Is my guitar too loud?*"

   Regardless of their response, say:

   "*My guitar is SUPPOSED to be too loud.*"

- "*I have to say; you're taking this very well so far.*"

- "*OK, well, we'll just carry on anyway until we find one you **do** like.*"

- *"Don't forget folks we're a covers band so if at any point you don't like what you're hearing – remember we didn't write any of this s**t."*

Tuning-up

- *"Anybody here have perfect pitch?"*

(Crowd does not respond.)

"Great, then I'm in tune."

Good when tuning up OR at the start of a set.

- *"Oh s**t! It's in tune - and I had such a great joke."* (After tuning up)

Song Intro

You can really play up the "I wrote this song" or what this song's about angle:

- *"This song was inspired by my latest failed relationship."*

(Ideally look for a ludicrous song to link it to)

- *"I wrote this song during my latest tour."*

- *"This song helped me break out of writer's block."*

- *"This is a song about twisted love."*

- *"This is about a love gone wrong"* etc.

- *"I wrote this song while I was in liars anonymous."*

- *"I wrote this song during my affair with Madonna, which lasted about as long as this song."*

- *"I wrote this song while I was an intern at the Whitehouse."*

- *"This next song is about... oh, it's about 3 minutes long."*

- *"Excuse me if I get a bit tearful during this next song - I've been feeling upset lately because my wife's run off with my next door neighbour .. ..and boy, do I miss him!"*

- *"This song requires some amazing guitar work. And at no time do my fingers leave my hands."*

- *"We're gonna slow it down a little for this next number, give everyone a chance to dance cheek to cheek, or you could turn around and face each other if you prefer."*

- *"This next song I wrote last week after I heard it on the radio."*

- *"Let's have a little fun, I know you guys are going to like this next one."*

- *"You all like to Rock n' Roll right?"*

- *"This is a great song but it is quite hard to play. Starting it is OK, but all finishing at the same time is another matter all together!!"*

- *"This song is dedicated to Linda, our rhythm guitarist's dead fish."*

This kind of thing is great for a sad ballad about lost love etc – although it can be hard to play while laughing. Look through the lyrics sheets for something suitable.

- *"I'd like to dedicate this song to my ex. You know, I miss her all the time. But my aim is improving."*

- *"This song is one of my all time favourites."*

(turn to band member);

"How does it go again?"

or:

"What's it called again?"

An extended version of this is to go on and on for a few minutes about how the next song is one of your favorites that you've loved since you were little, how it has so much meaning for you blah blah blah....then turn to the other band members and say:

"So what are we doing next?"

- *"This is my favourite song that we do."*

(Repeat for c.4 songs in a row)

- If you're playing a sad ballad say something like:

  "Ah...the story of my life."

  As it rings out. Then after something totally different and unrelated, an up-tempo rock number for example, say the same thing.

- *"This is one we wrote that <u><insert the original band name></u> covered."*

- *"This next song needs no introduction....so I won't introduce it."*

Getting audience members up

- *"Now, we need some help with a little extra rhythm here. Would anyone like to volunteer or do I have to come down and find someone?"*

- *"I need someone really bad. Are you really bad?"*

  (Talking to the person, on mic)

- To band mate as warning when you get a female up:

  "Don't be sexist. The birds hate it."

- If you're female and get a man up, try this to your female band mate:

  "Careful with the jokes we don't want to threaten his sexuality."

Band member introductions

- *"..And on bass, ladies and gentlemen, we are lucky to have probably the finest bass player in the whole of the <u>\<enter name of region / country\></u>. Unfortunately **he** couldn't make it tonight so we have <u>\<enter name of your bassist\></u>."*

- *"A legend in his own mind, on lead vocals..., <u>\<enter name\></u>"*

- *"The poster boy for goat abuse, our (bassist / keyboard player) <u>\<enter name\></u>"*

- *"A big hand for our drummer, <u>\<enter name\></u>...the hardest working member of the band! Folks, he just doesn't know the meaning of fatigue...well, actually, there's only a few words he **does** know the meaning of!"*

- *"Someone in search of a meaningful overnight relationship, <u>\<enter name\></u>"*

- *"He may not be Fred Flintstone but he sure can make your bed rock <u>\<enter name\></u>"*

- *"With more front than Katie Price, <u>\<enter name\></u>"*

- *"This man always wanted to be somebody – well perhaps he should've been a little more specific, <u>\<enter name\></u>"*

- *"...and I'd like especially to announce that we are the only <u>\<enter town / region\></u> area band to feature an all gay rhythm section! Thank you!"*

- *"A woman who didn't do herself much good on her recent appearance in court. The judge said "you've been brought before me for drinking" to which she replied "great, let's get started", <u>\<enter name\></u>"*

- *"A man whose motto is: "Rehab is for quitters", <u>\<enter name\></u>"*

- *"A man who gave up alcohol last year – it was the longest 20 minutes of his life, <u>\<enter name\></u>"*

- *"He took up jogging just so he could hear heavy breathing again, <u>\<enter name\></u>"*

- *"A man who's motto was "Fight fire with fire" which probably explains why his career with the <u>\<insert name of town\></u> Fire Brigade was cut short, <u>\<enter name\></u>"*

- *"The man who replaced every window in his house before he realised his glasses were cracked, <u>\<enter name\></u>"*

- *"For him it's a night out, for his family it's a night off, <u>\<enter name\></u>"*

- *"He's been called rude, cold, egotistical, self-centered and arrogant. But that was only his family's opinion, <u><enter name></u>"*

- *"People tend to take an instant dislike to her. It isn't very nice but it does save time, <u><enter name></u>"*

- *"A man who, after all's said and done, usually says just that little bit more, <u><enter name></u>"*

- *"His idea of multi-tasking is to read while having a s**t, <u><enter name></u>"*

- *"She gave up being a writer because she couldn't stand the paperwork, <u><enter name></u>"*

- *"I can introduce her, but I can't guarantee her, <u><enter name></u>."*

Requests

- *"I had a very special request, but I'm gonna keep singing anyway."*

(This one is great when someone has come up to the front or side of the stage to speak to one of the band in front of the rest of the room).

- *"Thank you. We do take requests, so just write them down on the back of a twenty pound note/dollar bill and bring it up to the stage."*

- *"We've had a request for <u><enter song here></u>. We don't do that one but this is similar and has some of the same notes / chords in it."*

- *"We have a request, but the microphone won't fit up there love."*

(Look theatrically towards the singers' rear)

- *"We have an agreement with <u><insert artist name being relentlessly screamed at you></u>. We don't play any of his songs, and he doesn't play any of ours."*

Hecklers

- *"Don't worry mate, I'm an a**hole when I'm drunk too."*

- *"Hey, do I come to McDonalds and shout at you while you're working?"*

- *"Get back to work! Those glasses won't wash themselves, you know."*

- *"Oh, look, someone didn't get enough attention as a child."*

- *"Save your breath for your inflatable date...."*

- *"This is why I don't like bringing you to gigs Dad."*

- *"Listen to him; I thought alcoholics were meant to be anonymous."*

After/during a major mistake onstage

- *"Don't you just love it when a song / gig really comes together?"*

Various

- Learn the names of the people working behind the bar and introduce them to the crowd during the performance.

  "For those of you who didn't know, Jenny is the beautiful brown-eyed bartender you see behind the bar. She's the one offering a slow comfortable screw for 2 pounds/dollars. This of course is a cocktail."

- Before you start your first set go to the venue toilets. Can you hear the sound system in the main room playing while you're in there? If so, dedicate a song during your performance to the guy or anyone who's on the toilet.

  "We know you can hear us..."

- Look around for distinguishing features to comment on. Like if there's a gigantic deer head mounted on the wall, say:

  "That guy with the antlers up there has no taste in music. He hasn't clapped for any of my songs so far."

- If one of the band members says something stupid try:

   "This is a special gig for <u>＜enter name of offender＞,</u> it's their last one with a mic."

-   *"I have the body of a god..... Buddha."*

-   *"In honour of all you beautiful people, everybody take a drink."*

-   *"In honour of our lovely waitress/bartender, who deserves great tips, everybody take a drink."*

-   *"Tips are greatly appreciated. I'm trying to help get my drummer's mom's moustache removed, so every little bit helps."*

-   *"Message to the owner of a lime green hearse: You've left your lights on."*

   (Works best as a random shout out followed by one of your band members leaving the stage.)

- If you're lead vocalist and playing the guitar solos, sing up to the solo in a song, then yell out:

   "Play it, <u>＜insert your first name here＞</u>!

   ...and then play the solo.

- After a slow dance number, tell the singer;

   "That was pretty awful......I mean awful pretty."

- *"Our fan club was supposed to come tonight, but they couldn't make it. One guy is sick and the other guy had to work."*

- To overly enthusiastic member of audience who may be yelling out etc:

    "Thanks, Dad/Ma." (as applicable)

- *"I haven't spoken to my wife for 18 months – I don't like to interrupt her."*

- *"The chef in here does a marvellous job for a man with his skin condition."*

(Use this with caution and never when you're playing a new venue or you know they don't have a sense of humour)

- *"I've eaten in here. The chicken was so old they had to bring it to my table in a wheelchair."*

(same caution advised here clearly)

- Muttering to yourself in a way that seems under your breath or almost off mic can go down well. The crowd will often quieten down themselves to hear what's going on. For example, if you make a normal comment that falls flat you can mutter something like:

    "That's the last joke I buy from a German!"

- *"The more you drink the better I sound. Please drink heavily."*

- *"The landlord has a special promotion on tonight of "Buy one get one free". Well that's what I think he meant when he told me to BOGOFF earlier."*

- Something else you can do is to Google *"This day in history"*. You'll generally find a couple of useful events you can incorporate into your act and mention on the night.

- *"Anyone having or just had a birthday?"*

People love to celebrate the birthday they had last week, or are having next month. Give them a name check which can also lead into something like:

"Let's raise our glasses for <enter name>. We'll play this for you."

- If there's a really overly enthusiastic crowd member, ask them their name on mic. Then say something like:

"Lucy knows how to party/rock!"

It may sound cheesy but it will put Lucy (and her friends) on a high for the rest of the night and encourage others to let themselves go even more.

- Re: football on Sky earlier:

"For a minute or two we were in with a good chance. And then the game started."

- *"My doctor warned me against any unnecessary excitement. So I switched to supporting <enter rival football team>."*

100

- *"My wife constantly complains I never listen to her. Or something like that..."*

- *"How can you tell when there's a drummer at the door? He doesn't know when to come in."*

- *"How would Oasis change a light bulb? Exactly the same way the Beatles would."*

- *"I went to see Pavarotti once. I tell you this much, he doesn't like it when you join in."*

- *"What do you call someone who hangs around with musicians? – A drummer!"*

- *"We once had a large gay following but we slipped down a dark alleyway and lost them."*

- *"Remember: there's a fine line between true love and a conviction for stalking."*

- *"If you're wondering how we play so well when we're pi**ed – it's because we practice when we're pi**ed."*

- *"Are you dancing or looking for your keys?"*

Show Close

- *"Thank you, you have been the best audience we have played to tonight."*

- *"If you would like to be put on our email gig list, please come up and give me some money so I can buy a computer."*

- *"If you have enjoyed yourselves tonight, we are <u><band name here></u> and you can visit us online at <u><web site></u>. If you haven't enjoyed us, we are <u><another rival band></u> and you can visit us at the job centre."*

- *"This is our most requested song. It's our last song."*

- *"Remember folks; if you're drinking, be careful on your way home. I'd hate to think of anyone hitting a speed bump and spilling the lot."*

- *"You've been a great audience...thank you both."*

- *"Remember folks there are 7 deadly sins. That's one a day so no excuse for not having a great week."*

- *"And now, in response to a number of requests we've received...goodnight!"*

Your own ideas for stage banter and one-liners

How you can put it all together

I hope you're now in no doubt that you or your band can rouse any of the crowds you play to. Turning even the smallest gig into a memorable event and connecting with every audience you play to aren't results that *just happen* though.

The fact that you've read this far means you have the desire to create a real presence when you play and, believe me, a strong desire is more than half the battle.

Don't get fooled into thinking things have to stay the way they are. Anyone can learn to behave differently on stage. If it helps, think of your on stage persona who's able to stir up the crowds as someone totally different from the 9-5 introvert you may be. Think of yourself as an actor. After all, in many ways that's what we are when we step on stage.

As with any new skill you learn, your ability to interact with an audience will improve over time. The more often you get out there in front of your public and practise the techniques, the easier it will become. The easier it becomes, the more natural it will look and sound and the better the response you'll get. You can guarantee it.

You only need to be determined and to persist in putting into practise the ideas I've shared in the previous pages of *Rouse the Crowd.* If you do this, you can radically change how your audience perceives you and how much enjoyment they (and in turn you), get from your shows.

Come back to this manual from time to time as you begin to see improvement in your audience responses. This will help you keep the advice in mind until you're aware of what to do without even having to think about it. As I say to readers of my other manual, Gig-Getter, you'll develop the skills in much the same way as you probably did when learning to play. Can you remember how much of a novice you felt when you first picked up a guitar or sat at your drum kit? How much there was to try and keep in mind?

I wrote *ROUSE THE CROWD* because I wanted to help those gigging bands and musicians who don't feel natural showmen or women – to be able to do their material and gigs justice on stage. I wanted to write the kind of guide that my band desperately needed at one point. The kind of guide that wasn't there when we looked for it. All the things you'd otherwise have to learn through trial and error.

I didn't want to write a great big reference book that was difficult to wade through. I wanted *"Rouse the Crowd"* to be something you could pick up and start using immediately to get better crowd reactions.

Because this was written with other musicians in mind I'm always pleased to hear from fellow band members and performers. Please feel free to share your success stories with me via *gareth@gig-getter.com.* Tell me which sections of the manual you found most helpful and give me any feedback on how you put these ideas into action. Don't hesitate to offer your suggestions for improvement and do let me know if anything still confuses or concerns you.

Everything you've read here is tried, trusted and proven to create better crowd responses by the successful bands and solo artists that use them. There's no reason you can't use them to do exactly the same. But be aware of one thing if you're really going to go for rousing your crowds: It can be quite a shock to have audiences start "coming on" to you. Make sure you're ready for it – it can change the way you feel about playing gigs forever. Good luck.

Gareth Bird

Rouse the Crowd Checklist

You, like plenty of other musicians, might find that, even when you know what you should do on gig night, forget certain things from time to time. Here's a useful short summary which can act as a checklist. Just cast your eye over this list of 23 pointers as each gig approaches.

Pre-Gig

1. *Rehearse as if gigging and "handicapped" if necessary*

2. *Decide what level of interaction you want and what to avoid from your previous shows*

3. *Mentally rehearse your success at the gig through visualisation and affirmation*

4. *Structure and use a set list to minimise and capitalise on known trouble spots and to plan for interaction at the best moments in the gig*

5. *Consider getting all band members involved with the crowd and agree an outline plan*

6. *Choose some appropriate "one-liners" - in case you need them*

Gig-Night

7. *Move some furniture at the sound check*

8. *Find a mirror and contort your face seconds before going on stage*

9. *Keep your focus on "giving" a good time to the crowd rather than just "taking" their applause*

10. *Slow down and deepen your breathing*

11. *Loosen your muscles (especially shoulders, jaws, teeth and tongue)*

12. *Fake it 'til you make it (Think about the way you act, move and talk in other situations when you feel at your most confident and adopt these mannerisms)*

13. *Consider an alter-ego and enjoy acting the way they would for the night*

14. *Don't expect anyone to enjoy it if you don't look like you are*

15. *Amplify your movements and expressions*

16. *Smile*

17. *Make eye contact*

18. *Open up / remove or reduce barriers between you and the audience*

19. *Make sure you can be heard: Speak up, speak slowly and watch your mic technique*

20. *Look for receptive crowd members & "court" them*

21. *Get someone up on stage!*

22. *Consider making band member introductions*

23. *Mention your website, merchandise (if you're selling it) or next appearance at the venue (if you know it)*

I wish you great success at all your gigs. Believe me you **can** make this happen and rouse **any** crowd you play to!

Recommended Reading

If you'd like to explore some more of the key elements talked about in *"Rouse the Crowd"* including some of the publications mentioned in the manual, here are some books you might find of interest. All of them can be found at Amazon and most good bookstores where you can check out full details of the contents.

- **Creative Visualization** by Shakti Gawain (published by New World Library)

- **The Silva Mind Control Method** by Jose Silva (Pocket)

- **Miracles** by Stuart Wilde (Hay House)

- **NLP: The new art & science of getting what you want** by Harry Alder (Piatkus)

- **The Definitive Book of Body Language** by Barbara & Allan Pease (Bantam)

- **Notes from a Friend** by Anthony Robbins (Pocket)

- **Win the Crowd: Unlock the secrets of influence, charisma and showmanship** by Steve Cohen (Collins)

- **Awaken The Giant Within** by Anthony Robbins (Simon & Schaster)

- **Gig-Getter: How to get more gigs than you can play** by Gareth Bird (GBA)

INDEX

For the latest info about
developing your stage presence
and additional free monthly
gigging tips, go to:

www.gig-getter.com

Look out for this best-selling gig-getting guide for semi-pro or amateur bands and musicians **from Gareth Bird**

GIG-GETTER
How to get more gigs than you can play

- Why you don't need to attract or pay a music agency

- Secret ways to use information about other acts to get band bookings worth £000's for your own act - year after year

- How to understand and use your act's real strengths to get venues to book your band

- Where to find band gigs & how to approach potential venues

- Working out what to charge & how to get people to pay it

- How to get interested venue bookers to CALL YOU!

- Discover the easiest, cheapest & most effective ways of getting your band name known to venues

- Insider secrets to feeling confident as you sell your act to people

- When & exactly how to ask for repeat bookings - and how to increase your prices

- How to create a unique demo which gets noticed, listened to and acted on

- 3 simple questions that can get one band booking after another from people you've never even met

- Easy ways to get audiences to come to your gigs

"Filled with advice on how to market your band" - **Guitar Buyer Magazine**

Get more gigs with Gig-Getter.....informative and practical steps to help any band get all the gigs they desire" - **Guitar Techniqiues Magazine**

"Covers everything from finding potential venues then successfully approaching them....to keeping venues sold so they book you time after time"
- **Performing Musician Magazine**

For more info visit - www.gig-getter.com